The Secret Garden

Written by Frances Hodgson Burnett

Retold by Fleur Hitchcock

Illustrated by Laszlo Veres

Collins

Chapter 1

Our carriage left the station in twilight. The horses clattered through a whitewashed village and plunged on until there were no more hedges and no more trees. Until there was nothing but a dense darkness on either side of us.

"This is the moor if you could see it," said Mrs Medlock from the seat beside me. "And that howling is the wind." We lurched along the track, bouncing from side to side, and I stared out at the darkness, not liking what I saw, not liking what I heard. It felt as if we were crossing a wide black ocean, broken only by the wind, the rain and the little streams that roared beneath the bridges.

It was so wild. So unlike my old home in India.

"So what do you think about where you're going?" shouted Mrs Medlock over the noise. "About Misselthwaite Manor."

"Nothing," I lied. "Nothing at all."

"Well I never," she laughed. "What an unusual child you are, Mary Lennox." She looked away and I felt cross with myself for stopping her. I wanted her to go on talking. I was desperate to know more about what was going to happen to me. But I wasn't going to ask Mrs Medlock. That would be giving in.

After a while, she sighed and leaned across me, pointing towards a distant light. "There it is – your uncle's house. One hundred rooms for a man who's never there. Well, hardly ever, since Mrs Craven died."

I watched the distant light appearing and disappearing and pretended not to listen, but I was paying attention. I was already wondering about my mysterious uncle and imagining his house.

"There are gardens of course. And trees – and ..." she paused. "Nothing else."

The darkness slid past and the house drew closer. I imagined the dead Mrs Craven dancing like my mother used to, wearing lace dresses and filling the house with music until the music stopped and the lights went out. I almost felt sorry for Mr Craven, whom I'd never met. And then I thought of myself going to his big, empty house and wondered if I could belong there, and then I felt less sorry for him. And then I felt lonely.

And for the first time in my life, a little scared.

Chapter 2

The next morning I awoke in a room hung with gloomy paintings. By the fire sat a maid, blowing on some coals.

Her name was Martha. I asked if she was my servant, but she told me she wasn't my servant, and she wasn't there to help me dress. In India, people had always helped me and she obviously found it funny that I didn't know how to do up my own buttons.

I struggled with the clothing, and she talked about her family and how they all had to get on with looking after themselves. Finally, she told me about her brother Dickon, who roamed the moor charming its animals.

She also mentioned that somewhere outside was a garden that had been locked up for ten years, ever since Mrs Craven died. I wanted to know more, but I didn't want to seem too interested in what a servant said. So I did my best to lace the boots she gave me and went outside to look for myself.

I walked the gardens, finding frosted trees and frozen fountains. A small red-breasted bird flew past me and landed on a tree behind a high wall. I tried to find a way to the tree, but there was no door. While I was searching, I came across an old man digging in a vegetable garden.

The bird suddenly appeared again, landing on an apple branch right beside me, and sang a cheerful song.

"What did he do that for?" I asked.

"He likes you," said the man. "That robin wants to be your friend."

At the word friend, I felt warm and almost happy. The robin shook his wings and flew back over the wall into the tree I'd seen before. But when I asked the old man about the closed down garden, he told me to stop asking questions. He then slung his spade over his shoulder and stomped off.

At teatime, Martha told me that the old man was called Ben.

"Why did Mr Craven hate the garden so much that he closed it down?" I asked.

Martha sniffed. "Mrs Craven loved that garden. Ten years ago she fell from a broken branch in there and she was so badly hurt that she died the next day. Mr Craven changed after that."

I sat thinking, listening to the wind, and in that quiet moment, I thought I heard distant crying. "What's that sound?" I asked Martha.

"Just the wind," said Martha brightly.

I didn't ask her again, but it didn't sound a bit like the wind to me.

Chapter 3

The storm raged, so I couldn't go outside the next day. There was nothing to do, so I decided to explore some of the 100 rooms. I found miles of pictures and old sculptures, a cabinet of carved elephants and a family of mice living in a cushion. And I heard the crying again.

I paused, listening. It seemed to be coming from behind a tapestry. I was about to pull it back when Mrs Medlock opened a door along the corridor.

"Mary Lennox! What are you doing here? Go to your own room this minute," she said crossly, and she marched me back through the house.

****

After the rainy day came the sun. Small white clouds raced through the deep blue of the sky.

Martha told me she was going home for the day, and I told her that I wished I could go, too, and meet Dickon.

"I wonder what he'd think of you," she said.

"He wouldn't like me."

"How do you like yourself?" she asked curiously.

And I thought about it, not for the first time. "Not at all really."

12

I felt so lonely that day without Martha that I ran around the fountain ten times until I met Ben again.

"Spring's coming. Can you smell it?" he asked. As he spoke, the robin landed close by.

"Do you think the robin remembers me?" I asked.

"Of course," said Ben. "He remembers everything in the gardens."

"Even the closed up garden?" I paused. "The secret one?"

"Ask him," Ben said as he turned his back on me.

I wandered along, eventually stopping by a long brick wall. The robin appeared by my side, picking at the earth, as if he was pretending not to follow me. Was he becoming a friend? My very first friend?

He hopped and poked and dug all around the bottom of the wall. We were only an arm apart and I felt deeply happy. He stopped and pulled at a worm. As he did, I saw something. It looked like a ring of rusty metal. I put my finger out and hooked it up and with it came a key.

A rusted key.

Perhaps it's been buried for ten years, I thought. Perhaps it's the key to the secret garden.

Chapter 4

When Martha came back to work the next day, I was so pleased to see her, I asked her all about her trip home.

"They wanted to know about you. Oh, and I bought you a skipping rope." She handed me a rope with two handles.

I must have looked confused. "Don't you know what a skipping rope is? Here, I'll show you." Martha ran into the middle of the room and began to skip, faster and faster until she was red in the face. "You have a go," she said. "Do it outside."

I slipped the skipping rope into my pocket but something occurred to me. "Martha, that was your money. So – " The word felt strange in my mouth. I'd never said it before. "Thank you."

She blushed, and I left before I did any more embarrassing things.

I skipped, spending most of my time near to where
I'd found the rusty key. The robin kept pace with me
and swung from the ivy that grew over the top of
the long brick wall, whistling.

"You showed me where the key was yesterday.
Perhaps today you'd like to show me where the door is?"
I said to him, only half-seriously.

And like magic, a breeze lifted the ivy away from
the wall and I saw a doorknob and a keyhole behind
the leaves.

With trembling hands, I took the key from my pocket
and opened the lock.

Once through the door I stopped to wonder. The tall thorny stems of the lifeless roses stretched over the garden from wall to wall and tree to tree. They formed a grey haze, making the garden mysterious and unlike anywhere I'd ever been.

It was still, so still, even my friend the robin froze.

I stepped softly from the door, as if I might awaken someone or something. Passing under the thorny arches it seemed the plants were dead. Or maybe they were just sleeping.

I bent down to smell the earth, and saw tiny, bright-green spikes poking from the soil. So, not everything was dead. Using a twig I scraped away dried yellow grass and found more and more fresh spikes of green. Other tiny plants seemed to be coming to life all around the garden. As I prodded the soil in one corner, some little white onion things came out of the ground. I took care to plant them again, and when I finally went back into the house, I asked Martha what they were, without revealing where I'd found them.

"Bulbs," she said. "They come up in the spring."

"I wish I could see them come up," I said. "And I wish I had a little spade."

"Dickon could bring seeds and tools if you want. Let's write him a letter to ask him."

Martha ran to get paper, and I watched the fire and listened to the wind. In the wind's howl, I heard the cry again. A distant howl of unhappiness.

That was the third time. And I wondered just who it really was.

Chapter 5

The sun shone for nearly a week on my secret garden and me. Every day I went and uncovered more life, more tiny plants, more bulbs. I didn't want anyone, even Ben, to find me in there, although there was something about the old man that I liked. His grumpiness reminded me of my own, so when I wasn't in the secret garden, I looked for him in the vegetable patch.

I let him dig while I tried to think of a question that wouldn't give my discovery away. "When roses have no leaves and look brown and dry, how can you tell if they're dead or alive?"

"Look for new buds," he grunted. Then he stopped digging. "Why do you want to know about roses?"

I blushed. "I was just pretending to be a gardener," I said. He looked at me in a way that suggested he felt sorry for me.

A little later, I heard a peculiar whistling sound. I skipped along the paths until I found a boy, with cheeks as red as poppies and sky-blue eyes. He was playing a tune on a whistle to an audience of two rabbits.

As I approached he held up his hand. "Don't move or you'll scare them. I'm Dickon by the way, and you're Mary."

I felt as if I knew him already, and he spoke to me as if he knew me. It was strange that I didn't mind. "I've brought you tools and seeds." Just then the robin came and landed in the holly bush, singing its heart out. "He's calling to you; he likes you."

"Really?" I did so want to be liked.

"Definitely." He laid out the seeds. "Now have you anywhere to plant these?"

I felt the blush race up my back. I hadn't thought it through. Why would I need seeds without a garden?

I made a decision. "Can you keep a secret?" I asked.

"Of course," he said. "I keep the animals' secrets all the time."

"I've stolen a garden. Nobody wanted it, nobody cared for it, perhaps everything is dead in it, but they're letting it die and ... and ..." I threw my arms over my face and burst out crying.

"Hey," said Dickon gently. "I won't tell."

So I dried my eyes and marched proudly to the ivy curtain. I pulled it back and pushed open the door behind.

Dickon stared, his wide, red mouth open, stretching into a smile. "Mrs Craven's old garden. I never thought I'd see this place," he said.

"It's my secret garden," I said. "And I want it to live."

Chapter 6

When I got back for my dinner, I was dying to tell
Martha about Dickon. But instead she told me that my
uncle wanted to meet me.

Mrs Medlock swept me through the house and I felt
myself turn back into the silent child who had stepped
off the boat from India. We entered Mr Craven's study
and Mrs Medlock left, leaving me with a man who
had the saddest face I'd ever seen. His eyes stared into
the crackling fire as if they were looking for something.

"You're very thin, very pale. Do they take good care of you?" he asked quietly.

"I'm getting stronger," I said.

"Should you have a teacher – ?"

"Please, no!" I blurted out. "Please, I just want to be in the gardens – I don't do any harm – "

"Don't look so frightened," he said. "You can do what you like. Is there anything you want? Toys? Books?"

"Could I? Could I have a patch of earth?"

"Earth?" He stood and walked back and forth and his eyes grew kind. "You can have as much earth as you want. When you see a patch you like make it come alive. Now, I shall be away all summer. Run around and enjoy the garden. Goodbye, Mary."

That night the weather was wild and I couldn't sleep. Once again, I heard the crying. I took the candle from my bedside and followed the sound through the gloomy passages until I reached a place where I could see light shining under a door. Someone was crying in that room and it was quite a young someone.

I opened the door and found a boy on a bed, the palest creature I'd ever seen. He was wailing, not a cry of pain, but a tired, cross sort of cry. He looked at me with pale grey eyes. "Are you a ghost?" he asked.

"No – are you?" I said, walking closer.

"No, I'm Colin."

"Colin who?"

"Colin Craven. Who are you?"

"Mary Lennox. Mr Craven's my uncle."

"Come closer," he ordered, and although I would have refused, I was so curious to find this strange boy living in the house, I did as he asked.

"I didn't know you were here," I whispered.

"I didn't know you were here," he said. "I'm ill you see, so ill that I'll not live long and I can't bear to be looked at or talked about. So the servants don't tell anyone about me."

How strange, I thought, that this house should be so full of secrets and yet how wonderful that one of those secrets should be this strange boy. My own cousin. And then something occurred to me.

"If you hate being seen so much, do you want me to go away?"

"No, I'd think you were a dream if you went – don't go. Talk to me."

Trying not to seem too keen, I placed my candle on a footstool, pulled my blanket around my shoulders and sat down.

And we talked.

I told him about growing up in India. About my mother dancing and going to dinner parties, and about everyone becoming ill and leaving me alone. About being left an orphan. I told him about sailing to Britain in a boat, about coming across the moor for the first time. He told me that he had a hunched back and weak legs and never left his bed even though a doctor from London told them that he should have fresh air. But that he didn't like fresh air and no one ever made him do anything he didn't like because they were all scared of upsetting him.

"Everyone does exactly as I say," he said, "because by rights, I should one day be master of this house." I wondered just how someone could become so spoilt that they thought the whole world belonged to them.

"How old are you?" he asked at last.

"I'm ten," I said.

"So am I," he said. "My mother died ten years ago, just after I was born."

"That's when the garden was locked, and the key was hidden," I said, forgetting myself.

"Which garden?"

"Oh – a secret garden – I don't know where it is."

"I'll make them tell me. I want to see it!"

"No," I said. "Don't do that – it won't be secret anymore." And I explained to him that it would be much more exciting if I could discover it and take him there and we could bring it to life between us. He asked me to describe how I thought it looked, which of course I did. I never said that I'd already found the garden. I talked until his eyes began to close. I then picked up my candle and crept away.

Chapter 7

In the morning, as rain beat on the windows, I told
Martha that I'd found Colin.

"Oh no, Miss Mary!" she cried, "I'll lose my job!"

I promised her that it was nothing to do with her,
that I'd found him on my own and that instead of being
cross, he'd been pleased to see me.

Martha explained that no one really knew what was wrong with him. When Colin's mother died, Colin's father was so upset he had turned his back on his son. He was scared that Colin would die as well, imagined that the boy was ill and refused to love him. Since then, Colin had sat up there in his room on his own, having whatever he wanted, becoming more and more spoilt but also, more and more lonely.

"Is it true that he'll die?" I asked Martha.

She shrugged. "He never goes out, he never moves."

I was thinking about Colin and wondering about the garden when Mrs Medlock arrived.

"Master Colin's summoned you both!" she said, looking shocked.

A few minutes later, I saw Colin together with Martha. He reminded me of a young prince I'd seen in India. A prince who treated his servants just as badly. In my mind, I compared him to Dickon – they couldn't be more different.

So I told him about Dickon. I told him about Ben and the robin. We talked about the moor, which Colin had never visited, and then the gardens. Finally we laughed. We laughed so much that we forgot that I was an orphan from India and he a sick boy kept in bed for ten years.

In the morning, the sky was clear and the sun shone. I dressed myself before Martha came and ran down to the secret garden.

Dickon was there. The garden seemed to have grown because of the rain. We sat watching the birds build their nests and I told him I'd met Colin.

"I'm glad," said Dickon. "I knew about him and I didn't like keeping it from you. They say Mr Craven wishes Colin had never been born. Which is awful."

I wondered if my mother had felt that, too. If she'd never read to me or kissed me because she didn't really want me.

"Look at the garden," said Dickon, as we sat in silence, thinking of Colin, unloved in his dark bedroom. All the green shoots were taller and the roses had thick fat buds on their grey branches. "Being here would take his mind off dying, wouldn't it?"

"I've been wondering that myself," I said. "If he could keep this place a secret, perhaps we could bring him out here in his wheelchair?"

Dickon thought it a good idea, and so did I until I visited Colin that night.

"Mary Lennox, you're a selfish thing!" he shouted at me. "I waited all day while you talked to your wonderful Dickon and you didn't come and see ME." And he threw his pillow across the room.

I stood open-mouthed for a second, before swinging on my heel and marching out of his room. I marched all the way back to mine, swearing every step of the way that I wouldn't see him again.

I felt so furious that I almost forgot about Dickon and the green shoots of spring, but when I returned to my room, Martha was waiting for me with some books from my uncle.

I looked at them and my anger melted away. Instead, I pulled out a sheet of paper, and began to write a letter of thanks to Mr Craven. Colin could wait.

Chapter 8

I was awoken in the night by terrible wailing. Colin.
I covered my ears, but he was too loud. At first I was
frightened, but then I was angry.

"He ought to be stopped!" I shouted into the dark.
I flew along the corridor and the closer I got to him
the more my temper grew. By the time I reached his
room I was furious.

"You stop!" I said. "You'll scream yourself to death in
a minute and I wish you would!"

For a second he did. Lifting his blotchy face from the pillow, he stared at me in surprise.

"If you scream another scream, I'll scream too and I'm louder than you!" I shouted.

"But I've found a lump on my back. I'm dying!"

"Nonsense," I said. "Let me see." And I looked. "There's nothing there that isn't completely ordinary," I said. "There's not a lump as big as a pin and if you ever say there is, I'll laugh! What you need is fresh air!"

Colin's sobs quietened and he reached out his hand. "Mary, stay with me so that I fall asleep to you talking."

So I did. I told Colin about the garden, and the roses and the robin building a nest. And I watched his eyes close until at last he slept.

The next day, after I'd been in the garden, I went back up to find Colin in his bed. "You smell of flowers and fresh things," he said. "Have you been with Dickon again?"

I told him I had. And I decided to tell him the truth. "I've found the secret garden. I found it weeks ago, but I daren't tell you. I can trust you, can't I? You can keep a secret? If you can, I'll show it to you"

For the next few days, Colin kept the secret, but he didn't see the garden because the weather was wet. At last, when the rain stopped, we were ready to carry Colin down through the house and into his wheelchair.

Dickon and I wheeled Colin into the garden and stopped by the curtain of ivy.

"Here it is," I said.

And before Colin could speak, Dickon pushed him through the door, and into the garden. For a long moment, Colin stared. I felt the garden with his eyes and ears, as if seeing it for the first time myself. Spotted through the grass were the seeds I'd sewn, all grown up into tall plants, bursting with blue and purple flowers. Over our heads the trees showed pink and all around us the scented roses blushed, butterfly wings fluttered, insects hummed. My garden was beautiful.

"Oh!" cried Colin, his cheeks almost pink. "Oh!"

Chapter 9

Dickon and I worked all that day, bringing flowers and fresh leaves for Colin to look at as he sat under the blossom in his chair.

"That tree there is dead, isn't it?" Colin pointed at a grey tree with a broken branch.

"Yes," said Dickon, and he had sadness in his eyes. "But the roses will cover it soon, and then it'll be the prettiest of all."

"I wonder how the branch broke," I started, and then remembered the story that Martha told me about Colin's mother and stopped.

Later, as the sun faded, Colin said, "I don't want this afternoon to end. But I'll come back every day to see the garden grow."

"Soon we'll have you walking and digging like us," said Dickon.

"Walking? Really?" asked Colin. "But my legs are weak and they shake when I try to stand. I'm afraid of using them."

"When you stop being afraid, you'll be standing and then you'll be walking," said Dickon, smiling.

"I shall?" Colin looked around as if he was looking at the garden for the first time. Then he lay back in his chair and stared up at the sky. We were quiet for a while until he suddenly said:

"Who's that man?"

I looked to see. It was Ben hanging over the top of the wall, shaking his fist at me, red faced and furious.

"You!" he said. "You dreadful girl! What are you doing in there? Mr Craven'll be furious with me!"

"It was the robin that showed me the way," I said quickly.

Dickon and Colin came forward and I saw Ben's jaw drop at the sight of Colin. His face turned from red to white in one instant.

"Do you know who I am?" demanded Colin.

"Yes," said Ben, his voice trembling. "You've your mother's eyes. You're the poor sick child."

Whether it was Ben's pity or Colin's own frustration that gave him strength I'm not sure, but Colin tore at the blankets covering his legs. Then, grabbing Dickon's arm, he pulled himself up until he stood beanpole straight on the grass, his head thrown back and his eyes flashing lightning.

I looked back at Ben. Much to my surprise, I saw a long tear slide down his cheek.

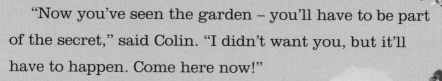

"Now you've seen the garden – you'll have to be part of the secret," said Colin. "I didn't want you, but it'll have to happen. Come here now!"

"Yes, sir, yes." And Ben climbed down the ladder behind the wall.

When Ben came round, Colin and Ben stared hard at each other, each measuring the other.

"What work do you normally do in the gardens?" asked Colin.

"Well, it was your mother that took me on. I used to do this garden years ago. In fact, I've been in now and again to look at the roses."

"I did wonder," said Dickon. "They'd have been in a much worse state if they'd been left alone all this time."

"That shows that you can keep a secret," said Colin thoughtfully.

There was a long, awkward silence. "Would you like to plant a rose, Mr Colin?" asked Ben in the end. "I've got one in the greenhouse."

When Ben came back with the rose, Dickon dug it a deep, wide hole. I watched as Colin touched the earth and his hands shook as he lowered the plant into its new bed. We all patted the soil flat around it and Colin stood back, his face pink in the sunset's light, his skinny legs wobbling, and laughed with joy.

Chapter 10

As Colin watched the garden change, so I watched Colin. He was still terribly rude to everyone, but over the summer he softened, strengthened and learnt. Just as I did. We began to understand the ways of plants and animals. And we learnt more about Colin's mother, how she'd loved the garden and the roses in particular, and how she'd loved the blue sky.

One day, when the bees were buzzing and the flowers were tall, Colin made an announcement. "I'm going to walk around the garden!"

So we formed a parade behind him, as if he really
was a prince. We were slow, and we stopped to rest
now and then, but fresh air and exercise had made Colin
strong, and his fear had almost gone. "What will my
father say when I walk into his study!" said Colin.

"He'll think he's dreaming," I said.

"This must stay our secret," said Colin. "I want to
walk into the house when my father's home and
surprise him – surprise everyone."

One day, towards the end of summer, the sun shone
hotly in the garden. We sang and we played and we
raced each other, so much so that Colin burst out of
the garden door into the garden outside. I heard him stop
and a voice say: "Who? What? Who?" as I pulled myself
to a halt just before bumping into the speaker myself.

Mr Craven.

This wasn't what Colin
expected. It wasn't what
I expected. I suspect it
wasn't what my uncle
expected. But when I
looked at Colin gazing
up into his father's eyes,
with his sun-browned face
and long legs, my heart
nearly burst with joy.

"Who are you?" said
Mr Craven again.

"Father," said Colin.
"You won't believe it;
I hardly believe it myself.
I'm Colin."

"Colin?"

"Yes, it was the garden that did it. No one knows. We kept it secret, all of it. Aren't you glad, Father?"

Mr Craven held Colin for a moment. He couldn't speak. He was overwhelmed to see his ill son suddenly so full of life. At last he said, "Take me to the garden, my boy. Show me, and tell me all about it."

And so we led him in.

The place was a wilderness of autumn gold and purple and violet blue and flaming scarlet. Lilies stood proud under branches of late roses and the sunshine deepened the colours, making the garden glow.

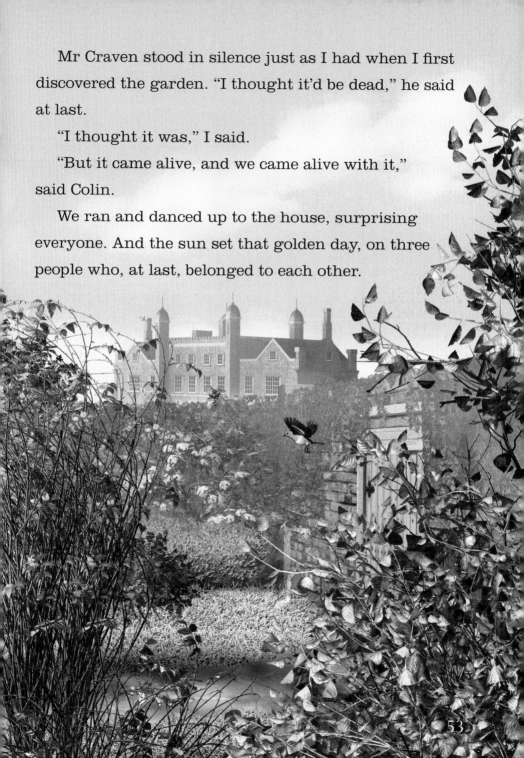

Mr Craven stood in silence just as I had when I first discovered the garden. "I thought it'd be dead," he said at last.

"I thought it was," I said.

"But it came alive, and we came alive with it," said Colin.

We ran and danced up to the house, surprising everyone. And the sun set that golden day, on three people who, at last, belonged to each other.

Mary, Mary, how does your garden grow?

Ideas for reading

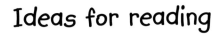

Written by Clare Dowdall, PhD
Lecturer and Primary Literacy Consultant

Reading objectives:
- check that the book makes sense to them, discussing their understanding and exploring the meaning of words in context
- draw inferences such as inferring characters' feelings, thoughts and motives from their actions, and justify inferences with evidence
- summarise the main ideas drawn from more than one paragraph, identifying key details that support the main ideas

Spoken language objectives:
- ask relevant questions to extend their understanding and knowledge
- participate in discussions, presentations, performances, role-play, improvisations and debates

Curriculum links: Science – living things and their habitats; Art and design – developing skills

Resources: digital camera; paper and pencils; gardening books/ICT; modelling materials

Build a context for reading
- Ask if anyone knows the classic story *The Secret Garden*, and to share what is known about it, e.g. characters, setting, events.
- Look at the front cover. Discuss what might be in the secret garden, and why it might have been locked up.
- Read the blurb to the children, and ask them to raise questions that might be answered through reading, e.g. why is Misselthwaite Manor mysterious? What has happened to Mary? Why is there a secret garden? Record their questions.

Understand and apply reading strategies
- Read pp2–3 to the children. Ask them to close their eyes and visualise the setting. Discuss which words and phrases help to create powerful images.